For Taylor, Lewis, Tegan and Brody,
Ellesse and Ebi-Rose, Ethan and Eryn.
With all my love, Nanny McFiz – EA

For Theia-Louise, may all your dreams sparkle – KH

First published in 2018 by Scholastic Children's Books
Euston House, 24 Eversholt Street
London NW1 1DB
a division of Scholastic Ltd
www.scholastic.co.uk
London – New York – Toronto – Sydney – Auckland
Mexico City – New Delhi – Hong Kong

This edition published exclusively for Scholastic Book Clubs and Fairs

Emma Adams

Unicorn
and the
Rainbow Poop

illustrated by
Katy Halford

SCHOLASTIC

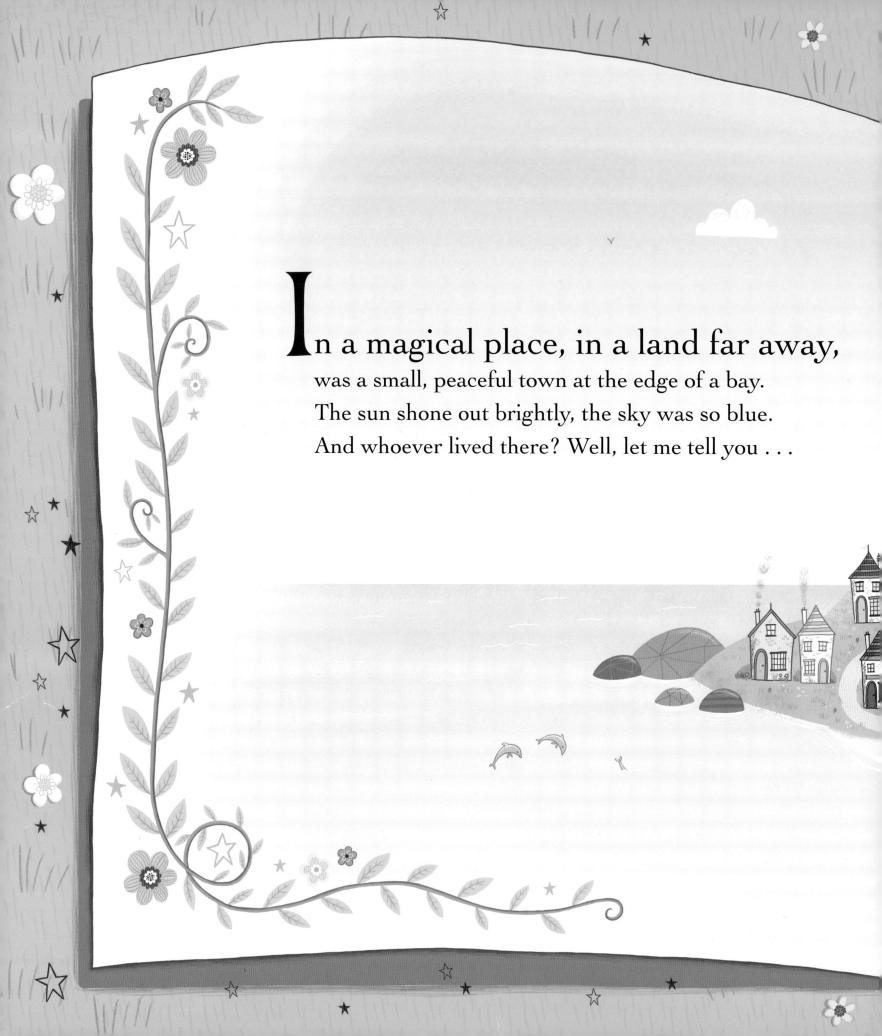

In a magical place, in a land far away,
was a small, peaceful town at the edge of a bay.
The sun shone out brightly, the sky was so blue.
And whoever lived there? Well, let me tell you . . .

There were . . .

Princesses (many),
big dragons (a few)

and witches (the good kind,
but some bad ones too).

Fairies with wings,
and birds fiery red.

WICKED WISHES

THE GLASS SLIPPER

WELCOME

PUMPKIN HIRE

And elves from the North Pole
who lived here instead.

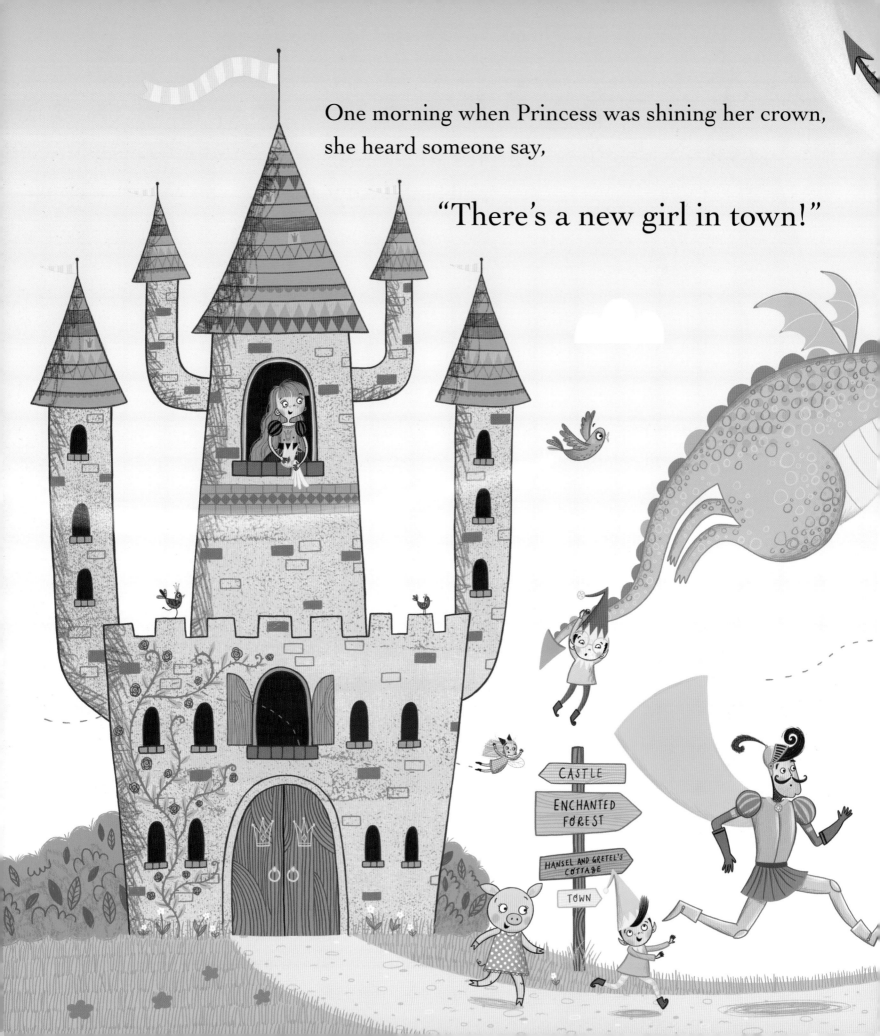

One morning when Princess was shining her crown, she heard someone say,

"There's a new girl in town!"

CASTLE

ENCHANTED FOREST

HANSEL AND GRETEL'S COTTAGE

TOWN

Everyone rushed to the forest (enchanted)
where Jack's giant beanstalk was long before planted.

They followed the "Neigh!"
and they pushed through the green.
To find . . .

. . . The best unicorn they'd ever seen!

The witches said,
"Welcome!"
then asked,
"Do you fly?"

But suddenly Unicorn seemed rather shy.
For just as the elves gave a loud, chorused

"WHOOP!"

the unicorn let out . . .

. . . A large rainbow poop!

Well! Now, let me tell you, this was a surprise.

The fairies all started to cover their eyes.

The birds disappeared and the dragons flew off.

All of the elves quickly started to cough.

"HOLD ON!"

called the princess (she needed to yell),

"Please tell me, just what is that . . . wonderful smell?"

She was right! There was something that smelled just like cake,

like sweeties and ice cream (the one with the flake).

And then they all realised
– it was very clear.
The **magnificent smell**,
it was coming from …

HERE!

As soon as the rainbow poop
touched to the ground
the most **beautiful colours**,
they spread all around.

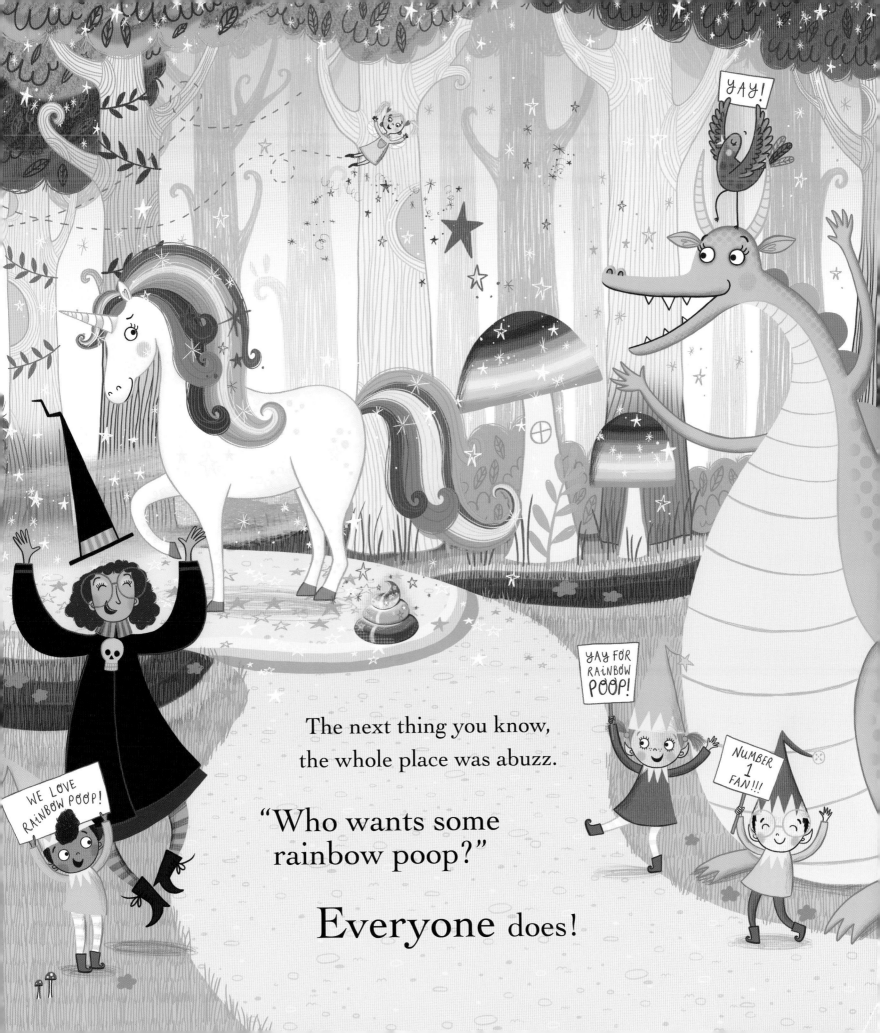

YAY!

YAY FOR
RAINBOW
POOP!

NUMBER
1
FAN!!!

WE LOVE
RAINBOW POOP!

The next thing you know,
the whole place was abuzz.

"Who wants some
rainbow poop?"

Everyone does!

It glistens like gemstones,
it sparkles like glitter,

it twinkles around all the birds as they flitter.

Somehow, the town had before looked much dimmer,

now everywhere Unicorn stepped seemed to shimmer.

The scent was **delicious**, the colours so **bright**,
"I love rainbow poop!"
shouted out Mr Knight.

TOWN

The townsfolk felt **giddy**, oh my what a sight!
This sweet-smelling rainbow was such a **delight**!

But . . .

FAIRY FROCKS

WINGS & WANDS

HUBBLE BUBBLE

Unicorn's smile had turned into a **frown**.
Her new friends were making her feel rather down.
She knew that her rainbow poop had caused a stir,
but everyone seemed to like **poop** more than her.

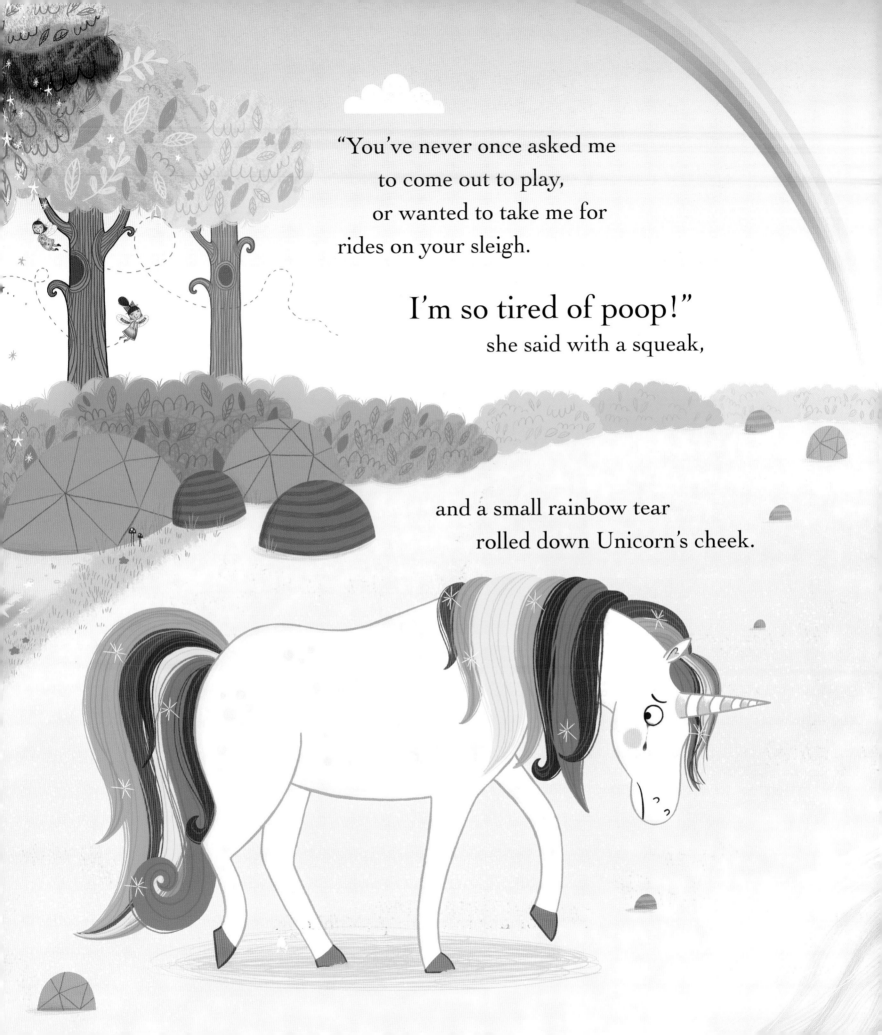

"You've never once asked me
to come out to play,
or wanted to take me for
rides on your sleigh.

I'm so tired of poop!"
she said with a squeak,

and a small rainbow tear
rolled down Unicorn's cheek.

Oh no – it was true! And they all felt so bad.
Their love for her rainbow poop had made her sad.

They planned a **big** party
and she had no clue.

then they all said a very
big, honest . . .

YOU!

Now **everyone's** happy, the sky's never grey
in this **wondrous** place, in a land far away.
They have **great** adventures, the fun never ends,
and Unicorn loves her **fantastic** new friends.

THE END